I Went to The End
Of The Rainbow

WRITTEN AND ILLUSTRATED

by

Pramita Chakraborty

MiddleRoad | Publishers

www.middleroadpublishers.ca

Library and Archives Canada Cataloguing in Publication

ISBN: 978-1-9991365-9-8
Illustration and words by Pramita Chakraborty
Book design by Ken Puddicombe

DEDICATED

to my son Deven, and curious little dreamers everywhere.

MiddleRoad | Publishers

www.middleroadpublishers.ca

I Went to The End

Of The Rainbow

Last night I couldn't fall asleep,
I opened one eye and took a peek,

A rainbow sat at the foot of my bed!

Curious, I tip-toed onto the red…

A festival of colours, sounds, and light,

Fireworks exploding into the night!

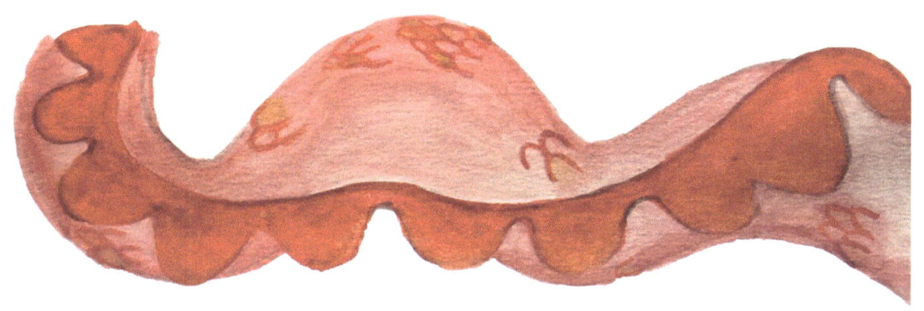

Paper dragons with a real live flame,

Curious, I stepped onto the orange lane…

I was flying over great dunes of sand,

With figs and dates filling my hands,

The sun's rays were deliciously mellow,

Curious, I hopped onto the yellow…

Silk-soft petals brushed across my face,

Bumblebees buzzed around in a race!

Mouthful of honey, sticky, and sweet,

Curious, I danced onto green street…

Monkeys passed me from tree to tree,

Bouncing along a great canopy,

Toucans, sloths, and a baby cockatoo,

Curious, I swung onto the blue…

Mermaids and pirates, all in a swirl,

A squid juggling eight clams and a pearl,

Turtles having tea-time in a treasure cove,

Curious, I dove onto the indigo…

Chocolate chip asteroids and a glass of Milky Way,

Martians, spaceships, and Jupiter sorbet,

A sundae topped with intergalactic whipped cream,

Curious, I leaped onto ultraviolet's beam…

Falling like rain to the ground,

I landed softly on a thundercloud,

I rode a lightning bolt to my bed below…

I made it!

I made it to the end of the rainbow.

ABOUT THE AUTHOR

Born in Dhaka, Bangladesh and raised in Toronto, Ontario, Pramita Chakraborty is passionate about discovering her own identity and celebrating her authentic self. She is and has always been an avid reader and artist. She believes that books make the best company and any piece of art, whether it is a doodle or painting, can tell you a lot about the creator. Pramita now resides in London, Ontario, with her family. This is her first published book, inspired by her own sleepless nights when she was pregnant with her son. She imagined reading this story to him and lulling him to sleep, with dreams of adventures to come.